Pickles

Pickles

Linda Yeatman

Illustrated by Valerie Littlewood

BARRON'S

New York

A percentage of profits will be donated to The North American Riding For The Handicapped Association, Inc. This organization, like The Riding for The Disabled Association described in *Pickles,* helps disabled children and adults to ride regularly.

First edition for the United States and the Philippines published 1988 by Barron's Educational Series, Inc.

First published 1986 by Piccadilly Press Ltd., London, England

All inquiries should be addressed to:
Barron's Educational Series, Inc.
250 Wireless Boulevard
Hauppauge, New York 11788

Library of Congress Catalog Card No. 87-35211
International Standard Book No. 0-8120-3955-6

Library of Congress Cataloging-in-Publication Data
Yeatman, Linda.
    Pickles / Linda Yeatman: illustrated by Valerie Littlewood.
        p.   cm.
    Summary: When Sarah is permanently disabled in an accident, she continues to ride the once-abused pony she nursed back to health and even enters a race.
    ISBN 0-8120-3955-6
    [1. Horses — Fiction. 2. Physically handicapped — Fiction.]
1. Littlewood, Valerie, ill.   II. Title.
PZ7.Y35P1 1988
[Fic] — dc 19   87-35211
                                                        CIP
                                                        AC

PRINTED IN THE UNITED STATES OF AMERICA
890   9770   987654321

Contents

FOREWORD

The story of Pickles and his owners, Sarah and Frances, describes only too well how disablement can so easily occur and how riding can help the disabled person, if not to complete recovery, at least to come to terms with their disability.

The Riding for the Disabled Association helps over 20,000 disabled children and adults to ride regularly throughout Great Britain and this story fairly indicates how this is done. For the majority riding is a new experience and a stimulating challenge bringing greater independence and happiness.

I hope that the readers of this story will appreciate the love and respect horse and rider have for each other.

HRH, The Princess Anne, Mrs. Mark Phillips

CHAPTER ONE

SARAH

Sarah was a determined child. "Obstinate" was the word her parents used. "Pig-headed" was what her brother William called her, while her teachers referred to her as "strong-willed." Some people might have thought her spoiled, but this was not the case, for it was not easy for her to get her own way. Her parents, on the whole, were strict. "Stupidly strict," thought Sarah, when it came to bedtime or not having ice cream cones when they passed an ice cream truck. She was the eldest of three children, and she felt that she always had to do what her parents told her, while her younger brothers, William and Michael, did exactly what they liked.

Sarah's strong will got her into trouble time after time. For instance, once she was climbing a tree and went higher

1

than was really safe just to prove she could get to the top. She had to be rescued by the fire department. "You're like a cat with nine lives," her father told her. "Take care not to use them up too soon."

When Sarah was nine years old, she decided she wanted a pony. She had visited the local riding school and she loved everything about it — the smell of the stables, the feel of the ponies, their warm breath when she stroked them, and their soft tongues as they licked her hands. "They're licking the salt off your skin," the owner said, as she saw Sarah's look of pleasure.

After a prolonged battle of wills Sarah was allowed to have regular riding lessons. "We can't really afford it," her parents grumbled, but they bought Sarah the hard hat she needed and some second-hand riding pants, and dropped her off each Saturday morning. She quickly made herself so useful that she was allowed to stay on and help for the rest of the day. She cleaned the saddles, filled haybags, mucked out the stables, and learned how to groom the ponies and pick up their feet and clean them so there were no stones lodged in them.

"Yuck, you smell of horses. Yuck, you smell bad," William used to say on Saturday evenings when she returned, but Sarah didn't care.

Sarah's family had to move when her father started a new job. Worse than losing the house she loved or changing school and leaving her friends, Sarah lost her Saturdays at the stables. For some time she moped by day and dreamed at night that she was back in the stables. It was at this point that she decided that if she owned her own pony everything would be all right.

She didn't say anything, of course, as she could imagine all the arguments her family would raise. How would they pay for a pony? Where could she keep a pony? Their new home was near the edge of a town.

"A pony can't live in our garden shed, or graze on our tiny lawn," she thought. "There must be somewhere, though, where it could live."

Frances, a girl in her class, invited Sarah back to her home one day after school. Sarah discovered she lived on the next street, and, what was more, at the back of Frances's garden was an old stable. It was dirty and filled with gardening equipment, but it could be cleaned out. Sarah took a big chance.

"Frances, why don't we empty one of the stalls in this stable? We could keep a pony here. Look, there's even a manger for the hay and a drain for the water."

"Keep a pony?" said Frances, astonished. "What a fantastic idea!" She was not sure if Sarah was joking or not, but if she was serious, it would be wonderful. Frances had always wanted a pony.

"We'll have to keep it a secret," Sarah said.

So, every evening after school, Frances and Sarah worked away, clearing and tidying until all the junk was in one stall, and the other stood clean and empty — for a pony.

When Frances's father came to get the lawnmower out he joked, "When's the horse coming?"

"Quite soon, Dad", Frances replied, and he laughed at his daughter's sense of humor.

It was a problem though. When would they get their pony? Where would they find it? How would they pay for it? And, what pony?

CHAPTER TWO

PICKLES

Several years before Sarah and Frances became friends, a foal was born on a hillside in Wales. It was a still June night, and in the shelter of some trees nearby the other mares waited, their heads drooping as they dozed. They could smell the new foal, but they merely flicked their tails and twitched their ears. Foals are usually born at night, and this was the season for birth.

As dawn broke, the new little foal, a colt, staggered after his mother. The green hills of Wales, green from the summer grass, stretched as far as he could see. As the days passed, his legs grew stronger and he learned to enjoy the freedom and space all around him. When the herd, led by his father, the stallion, galloped across the open hillside, the foal galloped, too, loving the speed and excitement. When the herd stopped to nibble the grass or stand in the shade, he would run and play with the other foals and yearlings.

There was plenty to see — butterflies and insects to sniff, bees seeking out nectar from the wild flowers. He had his nose stung once when he inspected a bee a little too closely. Other animals — foxes, rabbits and even a family of otters — shared the hills with them, and many birds made nests and reared their young there, too. Some sheep grazed on the other side of an old wall. The foals would lean over and snort at them, and then, kicking up their heels, they would rush away up the hillside again. The days were full and happy.

With September came the chill of autumn. The peace on the hillside was shattered one day when pickup trucks appeared from all directions. The herd galloped away, but still the trucks came on. As he galloped after his mother the young foal felt that his lungs would burst, but he ran until he was trapped with the other ponies in a small field. Trembling, the ponies turned and turned again, but there was no escape. His mother had seen it all before. "They won't take you away this time. They'll brand you, but you'll be allowed to stay."

She was right. The foals were cornered and had their ears clipped. They were then released on the hillside again with the stallion and the mares, while the two-year-olds were driven away. When the winter snow came the foal learned to welcome the trucks, for hay was thrown out of them for the ponies to eat in the bitter cold weather.

"That little bay pony is clever and strong," the farmer remarked, pointing to the little colt. "He'll make an excellent child's pony. But he's high-spirited and could be quite naughty if he is not properly handled."

For two years the colt ran free on the Welsh hills. When he was rounded up after his third summer, he was fully grown, alert and in great shape. He had rarely been touched by a human so he shied away violently when some men attempted to run their hands down his neck. For several days he tried to shake off the halter that was placed on him, but eventually he got used to it. He was totally unprepared for the shock, however, of being pushed into a large horse trailer.

One horror piled on another. He was driven to the autumn sales. When he was led around a ring he was tired, thirsty, and frightened, and so he laid back his ears and kicked out at everything that came within reach.

"Get over there," shouted the large man who had bought him. He had a harsh, unfriendly voice. Another trip in another truck, and the little bay pony was turned out into a

field with hardly any grass. Some bad-tempered old horses nipped him on the hindquarters and kicked out at him when he approached the food. As the long winter dragged on, he was always hungry, and his ribs began to show through his coat.

Life got worse, not better, for the little pony. In the spring his owners started to break him, but they were hard masters and he fought them all the way. He quickly became known as "the naughty pony."

"Let's call the little rascal 'Pickles'," someone suggested. And for the rest of his life he was known as Pickles.

He changed hands three times before he was five years old. With one owner he used to bolt, and stronger and fiercer bits were placed in his mouth, and then a sharp curb chain tightened behind his lower lip. It hurt him and frightened him so much he reared. On the day he toppled over backwards on to his rider he heard them say, "We must sell that pony."

The next owner placed a saddle on him that was too large, and he developed saddle sores where it rubbed his back. After that, he bucked and bucked whenever any child got on him, for the weight pressed on the sores.

"Use your stick on him," shouted a fierce-looking woman at the child. "Beat him when he bucks." But Pickles only bucked again.

"I'm not riding Pickles anymore," said the child.

Pickles became neglected, and the shoes that had been been put on him began to pinch as his feet grew. He stumbled continually and became lame. He was a sorry sight. No one would have recognized the handsome, lively little foal who had galloped so happily on the hills.

"Pickles must go before the winter," his owners decided. "Let's take him to the livestock sale next Wednesday."

CHAPTER THREE

A NEW HOME

It was the autumn school break.

"Let's go to the livestock sale up on Mill Road. It's not far," suggested Frances. "We'll see lots of horses and ponies there."

"Brilliant!" said Sarah. "We can even pretend we are buying one."

They noticed one man near them who was bidding for most of the cheaper horses.

"What do you want them for?" they asked him, but he wouldn't tell them

"Look," he suddenly proposed. "If I see a real cheapie, would you girls like me to bid for you? Name your top price." Frances shook her head, but Sarah told the man how much she had in her savings account. He laughed.

11

"You never know. Someone might be glad to get that for a pony."

At last Pickles stood, lame and dejected, in the sale ring. "What about that one?" the man asked. "I certainly don't want him. He's all skin and bones."

Before Sarah and Frances realized what had happened he'd bid for Pickles and bought him for them.

"Where's your money, ladies?" he asked.

"I'll be right back," said Sarah. "You stay here, Frances, and I'll get the money."

Sarah's mother thought she was at Frances's house, and so Sarah carefully crept in past her brothers who were slouched in front of the television and got her savings book. She cashed the money she'd been saving for just this moment and rushed back to the market.

"That was quick," said their new friend. "I've paid the sale officials. They tell me your pony is six years old, and his name is Pickles. Now, where's your transport? How are you going to get him home?"

"We'll lead him," said Sarah. "It's not far."

So, led by two excited girls, Pickles limped to his new home in a stable at the back of a town garden.

"Isn't he gorgeous!" said Sarah.

"Whatever are we going to feed him?" asked Frances, as they tied him up.

"I'll get Michael's hamster food," said Sarah. "I think there is some hay for the hamsters, too. And I've got a bag of pony nuts that I had before I moved."

Frances and Sarah kept their secret for nearly two days. By this time Pickles had eaten all the hamster food that Sarah had taken from home, as well as the pony nuts and all the hay that had been bought to last the hamster the whole winter.

"What are we going to do now?" asked Frances.

"Let's go down to the pet shop and buy some hay with our allowance," said Sarah. "We can bring it back in shopping bags. By the way, I'm a little worried about William. He complained last night that I am smelling of horses again."

"He will get a shock when he finds out he's right," Frances giggled.

While they were out, Frances's mother missed her plastic bowl and bucket from the kitchen. She thought her husband must have taken them for gardening, and went to look for them. When she opened the door of the old stable and saw a pony she nearly jumped out of her skin. "I hope they haven't stolen it," was her first thought. She ran her hands over his back and down his legs and noticed what poor condition he was in.

"Half-starved" was her word. Then she saw how badly his feet needed attention.

Just then, Sarah and Frances burst in, carrying some plastic shopping bags bulging with hay. They were almost more startled to see Frances's mother than she had been to see Pickles.

"Tell me where you got him," she asked Frances sternly. The girls told her how they had bought Pickles and how they had crept into the garden with him while she had been talking on the telephone. She laughted at their antics, and everyone felt better.

"Since Sarah paid for him, he's really her pony, but someone will have to pay vets' bills, blacksmiths' bills, and buy the food. Let's go around to Sarah's house and talk about this now."

The meeting with Sarah's parents was not half as bad as

Sarah had feared. It was agreed that Pickles would be owned jointly by both families.

"But you two girls must do all the work," insisted Sarah's father. "Riding will be out of the question until his lameness is cured. We'll solve the problem of saddle and bridle and where to ride if he gets better."

The vet was extremely helpful. "Nothing much wrong here that food and rest won't cure. You seem to have bought an excellent pony." He insisted that Pickles's shoes be taken off and his feet cut down and looked at regularly.

"I know a farmer with a paddock very near to your homes where Pickles can live. You've bought a Welsh Mountain

pony, and all mountain ponies need a bit of space," he told them. Sarah was speechless with happiness as she heard all this being arranged.

"Oh, Pickles," she said, when at last she found her tongue, "Oh, Pickles. We'll make you well. You'll be the loveliest pony in the whole world. We'll show them, won't we!" and she hugged his neck and buried her face in his mane.

Pickles was more interested in the pony nuts in Sarah's pocket than in being hugged, but he recognized he was among friends and inclined to agree with anything they said.

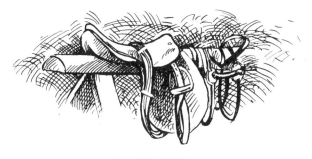

CHAPTER FOUR

BUCKING

After some weeks, Pickles looked better and was no longer lame. The blacksmith recommended keeping his feet without shoes for a little longer, which was disappointing, as Sarah and Frances longed to take him out of the field and ride him.

"I am not going to wait," Sarah decided, and some evenings, after filling his haybag and giving him his feed, she used to sit on his back.

"I'd rather hold the halter and leave the riding to you," Frances said. She was happy to lead Pickles and Sarah around the field, though.

What happened during the Christmas holidays, therefore, was totally unexpected. A secondhand bridle and saddle were bought.

"We'll all come down to the field and help you ride Pickles for the first time," said Frances's and Sarah's parents. Needless to say they knew nothing of Sarah's bareback rides.

"You go first, Sarah," said Frances, after Pickles was saddled up, and Sarah climbed on confidently. But as soon as Sarah sat on the saddle, Pickles bucked her off.

The parents were horrified. Sarah got to her feet and mounted again. Once more Pickles became a bucking bronco, and before Sarah knew what had happened she was on her back in the mud.

"You are not to ride that pony," her parents ordered. "He must be sold at once."

"Let me try bareback," Sarah pleaded, but her parents refused. Frances's mother examined Pickles's back very carefully and found signs of the scars from the old saddle sores.

"I don't believe you'll ever stop him bucking, Sarah," she said. "He must associate pain with being ridden. Your parents are right. We should sell Pickles now and then we can buy a pony that is safe for both you and Frances to ride."

She was wasting her breath. Both girls loved Pickles too much now to contemplate selling him.

"I won't sell him," said Sarah, obstinately, "I won't, I won't."

The following day, by sheer persistence, Sarah persuaded her parents to let her try riding Pickles without the saddle.

18

He was fine. "The bridle doesn't worry him. "Let's try the saddle again," she suggested.

As soon as Sarah sat on the saddle Pickles became unrideable.

"We need time," Sarah told Frances. "Time to improve our riding, and time for Pickles to forget the pain of being ridden with a saddle."

A few days later a friend of the farmer, named Mrs. French, telephoned. "I've seen your pony in the field," she told Sarah. "Could I possibly try driving him? I have a little cart and some harness. He might make an excellent driving pony."

Sarah and Frances talked it over and called her back. "We agree to your trying Pickles in harness," they said, "so long as we can always be there. He has been cruelly treated before, and we don't want it to happen again."

At first Mrs. French was annoyed at the suggestion that she might be cruel, but then she laughed. "I haven't been spoken to like that by children before, but you are quite right. He's your pony, and you don't want any more damage done. By all means come along. You might be able to help me."

Mrs. French was good with horses, and, using her voice to steady him, she put on the harness and backed Pickles between the shafts of the little cart. At first she only made

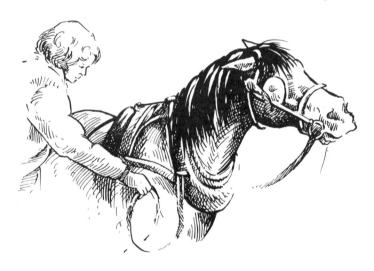

him walk a few paces. When Pickles felt the weight pulling behind him his ears went back and he started to kick out. Then, with Sarah and Frances, one on each side of his head, he was led quickly forward again. His ears went back, but he accepted the weight. Once around the field was enough for the first time, and he was given his feed.

For the rest of the holidays Sarah and Frances worked with Mrs. French. Pickles learned quickly and after a few days seemed quite used to pulling the weight of the cart. Soon he would walk, trot and canter, turn and stop. Mrs. French always used her voice for commands. Her touch on the reins was light, her voice encouraging, and she never used her whip.

"I think we can take him out now on some country roads to build up his fitness," she said.

Pickles enjoyed these drives. He lifted his feet well as he trotted out with the little cart behind him. There was room for Sarah and Frances to sit with Mrs. French, and very occasionally she let them take the reins.

"I would really like to buy Pickles. Would you sell him to me?" Mrs. French asked once, but when she saw the look on the girls' faces she knew she had made a mistake, and she never mentioned it again. In April, though, she did ask their permission to enter him for driving competitions.

"He's so quick and neat, I believe we could win prizes all over the country," she announced.

With Mrs. French's help Sarah and Frances now tackled the problem of riding Pickles with a saddle. Sarah still rode bareback in the field as often as she could, and he never bucked.

"We'll use this sheepskin between the saddle and his back," Mrs. French explained, "and then he won't feel the same pressure. The next step will be to get him used to having some weight on the saddle."

So Pickles had the saddle put on with a soft fleecy rug beneath it. Next, a sack of potatoes was laid across the saddle. Pickles bucked. The potatoes flew off.

"Steady, old boy, steady, Pickles," they said, and the potatoes were replaced. Pickles quivered, and his ears went back, but he did not buck. Before long, Sarah and Frances could lead Pickles around the field with the potatoes on the saddle.

When Mrs. French decided Pickles was ready for Sarah to mount, Frances and Mrs. French held him. He did not buck.

"Walk slowly around the field, as you do when you have no saddle," said Mrs. French. Sarah walked him around the field, then slipped off and gave him some pony nuts. Before long Sarah was able to walk, trot, and canter around the field.

Now came Frances's turn. She was much more nervous than Sarah. "Do you think he will feel how frightened I am?" she asked. But it was almost as if Pickles understood that he had to take extra care of Frances, and he allowed himself to be led gently around with her on his back. Frances was ecstatic.

"That was wonderful, Pickles," was all she said as she slipped off and hugged him.

CHAPTER FIVE

SUCCESS

Throughout the summer Pickles's life was busy. Mrs. French practiced driving in and out of cones and through obstacles in preparation for the driving competitions, and Sarah and Frances rode most evenings after school.

The blacksmith always took a lively interest in Pickles. "Why don't you join the local Pony Club?" he asked when they took Pickles to have his shoes changed. "You'll learn a lot there, and so will the pony."

He gave them the name of the local organizer, and in July, Sarah, Frances, and Pickles attended their first Pony Club rally. At first Pickles was nervous and tried to kick some of the other ponies, and their riders were quite rude in return. But the instructor was helpful, and Pickles soon settled down.

At the end of the afternoon they practiced some simple gymkhana events. Sarah and Frances had never done any bending races, but Pickles had learned to weave in and out of the cones when he was being driven by Mrs. French. Quick as a flash he darted in and out of the posts, leaving the other ponies well behind. Now the other riders looked at Pickles with new respect.

"Potato race next!" called out the instructor. Pickles had never before collected potatoes off the top of posts and taken them to a bucket, but he was extraordinarily quick to learn, and raced up and down from post to bucket. The whole Pony Club roared with laughter when he picked up a potato in his mouth that Frances had dropped and let it fall into the bucket.

"You've got a genius of a pony there. We'll be winning all the local meets with Pickles," Sarah and Frances were told. They were very proud.

The day of the first driving competition arrived. Sarah and Frances were to take turns on the back of the cart, which had been painted and polished until it gleamed. They had been worried about Pickles going in a horse trailer, but with practice he had gotten used to it. Now, at the show, they viewed the other competitors with alarm. Horses and ponies, carriages and carts of all shapes and sizes were to be seen all over the showground. The brass band frightened Pickles when it turned up too close to the collecting ring, but once he was in the show ring he was superb, and they had a clear round.

"Come on, Pickles! Come on!" Sarah shouted, jumping up and down by the ringside as Mrs. French and Frances took him around again, this time against all the other competitors who had clear first rounds. He made a couple of mistakes, but they won the fifth prize and received a white rosette.

"That will be the first of many, you'll see," said Mrs. French, who was as excited as Sarah and Frances.

Every day something wonderful seemed to happen during the summer vacation. Either Pickles was winning prizes at the driving competitions or the girls were riding him. Frances became quite bold and confident and, like Sarah, enjoyed riding across the big fields after the harvest had been brought in.

"I have never been so happy," thought Sarah as she galloped across a huge field in the first week of September. As the air rushed past her face and Pickles's hooves thundered over the ground she felt exhilarated beyond belief.

"I hope life goes on like this forever and ever," she shouted in joy.

Pickles agreed.

CHAPTER SIX

DISASTER

Sarah's wish was not to come true. Only a few weeks later she was in a terrible accident, and her life changed completely.

She was waiting at a bus stop with her mother and William and Michael. A truck came around the corner, and its brakes failed. Sarah's mother saw the driver's terrified face as he tried to stop the truck and steer it away from the pavement. She pulled the boys aside but was too far away to help Sarah, who had her back to the road.

Sarah had no warning. One second she was talking, the next she was thrown in the air and flung against a wall. Other people were hurt, too. The ambulance came quickly and took them all to the hospital.

Sarah never remembered being hit by the truck. The first

thing she could recall after standing by the bus stop was bright lights all around her, and being told she was in the hospital. She had to go straight to the operating room, as she had a broken hip and a broken arm, and the X-rays showed some damage to her back.

"She is lucky to be alive," the doctor told her parents. "She will pull through all right now, but at the moment we can't tell how bad the damage is to her back. She might not be able to walk again."

"Sarah not walk!" gasped her mother. "It's not possible!"

"Poor Sarah," said her father, shattered by the news. "How could this happen to her?" Then, looking firmly at the doctor, he said, "You must do everything you can, and we will, too, because Sarah will walk again if she possibly can. I know Sarah."

"Not walk!" said Mrs. French when she heard. "That will mean no riding. Sarah won't accept that easily," and she, too, echoed the words, "Poor Sarah."

Everyone was very kind, and it was some time before Sarah began to take in what had happened to her. Frances came to the hospital every day and kept Sarah up to date with what was happening. Mrs. French continued to win prizes, and Pickles was becoming famous in the driving world. One afternoon when they were watching a horse show on television, Sarah saw Pickles on the screen.

28

"Look at Pickles," she shouted out loud in her excitement.
"Everyone, look at Pickles!"

*   *   *

"Don't waste your time with me, Frances," Sarah said
when she next saw her. "Spend the time with Pickles. I
know Mrs. French is taking care of him, but he must miss
us. Feed him, ride him, tell him I'll be back just as soon as I
can." She looked small and white in the hospital bed, but
there was a spark of the old Sarah.

She longed for Pickles to come to the hospital to visit her
as her family and friends did. "Can't you smuggle him in?"
she asked Frances, who giggled at the idea.

"I'd never get Pickles up three fights of stairs, and can you

see the faces of the hospital staff if I tried to bring him up in the elevator?"

Sarah tackled the floor nurse next, who didn't see anything funny in the idea. "A pony on my floor! You must be crazy, dear!" she snorted as she bustled off.

"Crazy," thought Sarah. "You are the crazy ones. We'd all feel much better on this children's floor if we had a few animals to love," and she made up a wonderful daydream about ponies bringing in the food trays, ponies taking doctors on their rounds, and ponies there just to hug and love.

*   *   *

Pickels missed Sarah, too. Where had she gone? Why had she stopped riding him?

Each day he waited by the gate for her. Sarah was in the hospital for many months, so he had a long wait.

Then, in the spring, a car drove up and Sarah's parents and Frances got out. Pickles pricked his ears, pawed the ground. Was that Sarah in the car? Why didn't she get out and come to him? Sarah's father opened the back door and lifted something carefully out of the car. It was Sarah.

Pickles whinnied with joy as two skinny little arms were wrapped around his neck. Sarah hadn't meant to cry, but tears streamed down her face as she stroked Pickles. Again and again she said, "Oh Pickles, I have missed you." All he could do in return was to hold his head down and nuzzle her.

"I meant to come and see Frances ride you, but I don't think I can bear it, Pickles," she sobbed. "Wait for me. I'll get better somehow, I know I will."

No one heard Mrs. French approach. "Coming for a drive with Pickles, Sarah?" she asked, as though it was quite normal to see Sarah there.

"Sarah's not well enough at the moment," her mother said, but Sarah's face lit up.

"Yes, Mrs. French. I'll come for a drive. Where shall we go today?"

This was the first of many drives with Mrs. French. Sarah had to be lifted into the cart, but she became quite expert handling the reins.

"What would I do without you?" she sometimes whispered to Pickles, as she gave him a tidbit to eat on their return.

CHAPTER SEVEN

DIFFICULT TIMES

"We'll have to sell Pickles. We can't keep him any longer," Sarah's parents told Frances's parents. "Sarah's never going to ride again, and it will only make her unhappy to keep him."

Frances was in despair when she heard this. "You can't sell Pickles. Sarah will die if you do," she cried. "Can't we buy Sarah's half and not tell Sarah?"

"We can not afford to keep him on our own," her parents told her. "The other problem is that Mrs. French is soon going to America for a whole year, and we could never manage to look after Pickles without her or Sarah."

Frances went to Pickles's field and told him all her troubles. He pawed the ground and trembled, for he could feel that everything was going wrong, but he didn't know

32

how to help.

Meanwhile, Sarah was trying to get used to a wheelchair so she could go back to school. There were many problems, one being the steps everywhere. Ramps were made, and Sarah managed to get around the school. But she had to turn the wheels with her arms and she got very tired.

At first her brothers were wonderful. "Look at this," William would say as he fixed up one gadget after another to help her do things from the wheelchair. Both he and Michael pushed her chair when her arms got tired from turning the wheels. But after a while they got bored and wanted to go off and play with their own friends. Sarah's friends, too, were helpful to begin with, but in time they

began to exclude her from their activities, all except for Frances, who was very loyal and patient.

Try as she might, Sarah could still get no movement in her legs. Sometimes, when no one was around, she would try to stand on her own. How humiliating it was to fall, and not even be able to get up by herself. One day Frances came in and found her lying on the floor, crying.

"Sarah, whatever is the matter?" she asked, her face wrinkled in concern.

"I can't do it! I can't walk!" cried Sarah. "I don't think I'm ever going to get better. Oh, if only I could ride Pickles again I wouldn't mind not being able to walk. Why did this happen to me?"

It was hardly the moment to tell Sarah that Pickles was going to be sold. For the last few weeks, since Mrs. French had gone to America, he had become increasingly frisky. The summer grass was strong and he was getting too little exercise. It had been agreed that he would be sold as soon as a good home could be found — "The sooner the better," was the parents' point of view.

Frances helped Sarah back into the wheelchair.

"If only I could think of something," she said to herself.

CHAPTER EIGHT

HILL FARM

Each week Sarah had physical therapy at the hospital. The doctors were doubtful she would get back the use of her legs, but the physical therapist did not give up hope. She did exercises with Sarah and gave her massages, trying to get some twinge of movement back into her legs. Sometimes there were signs that they might succeed.

"Have you ever done any riding, Sarah?" she asked one day.

"Have I ever done any riding?" echoed Sarah. "How can I possibly ride if I can't use my legs?"

"Have you heard of Riding for the Disabled?" continued the physical therapist, ignoring Sarah's rudeness. Sarah shook her head.

"There is a riding school not far away at Hill Farm. Each Saturday disabled children ride there. I might be able to get

35

you into the group. I'll talk to Joan, who runs it. She is a physical therapist like me. It might help you."

So the next Saturday Sarah's parents drove her to Hill Farm, where there was a small riding school. Sarah's heart missed a beat when she saw a string of ponies and children returning from a ride. It was so like the riding stable she used to go to.

A large woman brought up a pony. "Hello, Sarah! I'm Joan, and this pony is Nobby. If we lift you on, would you like to ride him?" she asked Sarah, kindly.

"I'll just fall off," Sarah replied, "but I don't mind."

"That's all right. We'll hold you on," Joan reassured her. "And here is a neck strap to help you."

"What sort of riding is that?" thought Sarah, but she said nothing. Her old riding hat was put on, and she was lifted on to Nobby. He was fat and docile, and stood quite still while Joan adjusted Sarah's stirrups. When they walked forward Sarah felt very strange, unsafe, but excited. Someone led Nobby while two other women walked on either side, holding Sarah's knees against the saddle.

"Come and join the others," Joan said to Sarah, and led the way into a riding school. From the middle she instructed five or six children, all with helpers. Sarah only walked, as she had no strength in her legs to deal with trotting, but she watched as the others trotted around the ring, and some of them cantered, too. It was really thrilling when one boy of twelve cantered for the first time without anyone holding his pony. At the end of the session they had bending races and potato races just like the Pony Club, and Sarah joined in with these.

All the children were disabled, but it was not until they dismounted that Sarah realized how badly handicapped some of them were. One or two had great difficulty walking to the cars, yet, when they had been on the ponies, they had seemed quite normal.

"Next week I'd like to ride Pickles here," Sarah

announced to Joan. She told her about Pickles and how wonderful he was.

"We can only use ponies that are absolutely safe for Riding for the Disabled, Sarah. These ponies here are not only ridden by this group, who are all intelligent children with physical disabilities. During the week children come from all around who are handicapped in other ways. The ponies must be totally reliable."

Sarah told Frances all about her ride.

"Do you think Pickles would be all right for Riding for the Disabled?" she asked. "He'd have to go and live at Hill Farm and be used by different people all the week. You may not want that."

"Perhaps I can go and talk to Joan," Frances said, hugging herself in excitement. A new home might be found for Pickles, and Sarah might be able to ride her there.

Frances talked her parents into going to Hill Farm with her, and she spent a long time talking to Joan. "Come and see Pickles, at least," she pleaded.

"Perhaps we can borrow him for a few months, and we'll see how he behaves," Joan suggested, reluctant to have a naughty pony at Hill Farm.

CHAPTER NINE

JOAN

Pickles was surprised when he found himself at Hill Farm. The other ponies were friendly on the whole and he enjoyed their company. It reminded him on his days with the herd on the Welsh hills. Nearly every day after school he was ridden, for many children, not only disabled riders, came to ride at Hill Farm. Frances came up regularly and had lessons.

"It's wonderful," she told Sarah. "Joan is teaching both Pickles and me so much. We've started jumping all those brightly painted jumps in the field. Pickles is terrific."

To start with, Pickles never went into the ring when the disabled children came, except for the session on Saturdays with Sarah's group. Sarah had gotten her way and was allowed to ride him, and Pickles took tremendously good care of her. It seemed a lifetime since Pickles and Sarah had battled over his being ridden at all. Now, with the special neck strap to give Sarah something extra to hold on to, and a halter under his bridle so he could be led by a helper, he and Sarah achieved a little more each week. The physical therapist noticed the increased strength in Sarah's legs. If Sarah noticed it, too, she didn't say anything.

Sometimes on Saturday afternoons Joan would say, "We're going for a ride in the country today." Sarah no longer needed people to hold her knees on to the saddle, but, as her legs were still weak, Joan would take Pickles by the leading rein on these rides. Other grownups came, too, to help.

"I love riding through the woods and around the fields," Sarah told Frances. "I never noticed before how beautiful the wild roses are, and the little flowers in the woods. Today the woodland tracks were dappled in sunlight. I noticed how pretty it was. I don't see these things much any more, as I have to go everywhere by car. I only really get outside when I'm riding."

A favorite ride took them past a pick-your-own strawberry field. "We'll stop here for a few minutes," Joan would say. "Let's enjoy ourselves." Then she'd buy some strawberries from the owners, and they would all eat them as they sat on their ponies.

"So different from the soggy strawberries from the supermarket," Sarah said to one of the other riders as she wiped strawberry juice off her face with the back of her hand.

One day it started to rain just before their ride.

"You'd better get back in the car," Sarah's mother said.

"Nonsense!" cried Joan in her loud voice, as she strode across the wet yard. "A little rain never hurt anyone. Come on children! Time to get on your ponies!"

In truth, all the children were glad, for apart from it being difficult to hold the slippery reins, they enjoyed being out in wet weather. They didn't get many opportunities to feel the rain on their faces.

In time Pickles began to help with the other Riding for the Disabled groups that came to Hill Farm. "He's so good with the epileptic children who come from a special school on Tuesdays," Joan told Sarah, "and the Down's Syndrome children who come on Thursdays."

At first Pickles was not sure what was going on when he helped with these groups, but he soon learned that if a neck strap was put on when he was saddled up and the halter left on under the bridle, then a child who needed special care would be riding him. He took great pride in going steadily when he was ridden by one of these children. They loved him for his warmth and even for his hairiness, and Pickles liked this.

His respect for the grownups who helped Joan week after week grew. Whatever the weather they were there, holding children on to the ponies, running beside the ponies as they trotted or even cantered, putting the ponies out in the field afterwards. But they shared the triumphs of a child who could at last, after years of bumping, rise to the trot, or a child who could finally steer a pony in a figure eight in the center of the ring.

"There is nothing glamorous about this," Pickles thought, "but a lot of hard and muddy work. But they know how much most of the children enjoy it."

Since Mrs. French had been in America, Pickles had had no practice at driving. But not far away was another farm where special driving lessons were given to disabled people. Joan agreed that they could borrow Pickles once a week. He used to go in a horse trailer and be harnessed to a little cart that had been built for disabled people.

On one occasion he went with this group to a large park where a big international driving competition was being held. Over forty groups of Driving for the Disabled were represented. Pickles trotted proudly around the ring, ears pricked.

"Special commendation to Pickles, the Welsh Mountain pony," rang out over the loudspeaker. "If more groups could have carriages made for the disabled and ponies like Pickles to pull them, many more disabled people could enjoy driving," the commentator announced.

Pickles was proud. Now he was not only helping Sarah, he was helping the other disabled children who rode him, and some disabled drivers.

His picture was in several different newspapers the next day. Sarah and Frances cut them all out and sent them to Mrs. French in America.

CHAPTER TEN

VACATION

"There's a Riding for the Disabled vacation in August, Sarah. Would you like to go with Pickles?" Joan asked.

Sarah discussed it with Frances. "Every disabled rider is to have the use of a pony for a whole week, and everyone is to have an able-bodied helper. Can you come and be my helper? Then all three of us can go."

"It sounds terrific," Frances replied. "I'd love to. I heard Joan talking about it. It's in Wales, and there are all sorts of things to do there."

"You know we were all going to have a vacation together? Perhaps we can have it in Wales after the Riding for the Disabled vacation." Sarah suggested.

Their parents were able to rent an old farmhouse near the Riding for the Disabled Holiday Center and planned to go there with William and Michael while Sarah and Frances and Pickles were there on the riding vacation.

"Pickles can stay on for a second week and be the pony for another child and able-bodied helper," Joan arranged, "then you can all travel back together."

Pickles went to Wales in the horse trailer with another pony from Hill Farm. Sarah and Frances rode in the front. It was a long trip, but when they arrived, it was the most beautiful place the girls had ever seen. A noisy river rushed past the hostel where the children were to sleep, and there were hills all around. The ponies were stabled in a huge barn. Meals were eaten in the hostel, and everyone had to help with something.

Sarah had her wheelchair with her, but she was beginning to use it less and less. Walking was difficult and painful, but, by holding on to the furniture, she could pull herself around. They slept in bunk beds. "You have the bottom bunk and I'll have the top one," Frances told her.

"It is almost as if I had never had the accident," Sarah told her one night. "Everyone here is so warm and friendly, and no one seems to mind whether we are disabled or not."

Riding obviously formed a major part of the day for all the children. There was hiking, riding in the school, competitions, and treasure hunts. In between there were outings, picnics and barbecues, movies, and games. Most evenings ended with songs around a fire. Sarah talked to some of the children who were much more disabled than she, and with no hope of getting better as she was, but there seemed to be no bitterness in them. It was as if by being handicapped they concentrated more on their advantages, such as a greater sense of fun and laughter. The week passed quickly for everyone.

Sarah's mother came to drive Sarah and Frances to the family vacation.

"The house is up this road," she said, as the car bumped up a stony road to the old farmhouse they had rented. Hidden in a fold in the hills was a small valley with a stream, and only one old stone house. Sheep wandered around freely, nibbling the grass right up to the front door. On the other side of a stone wall, a herd of Welsh ponies grazed.

"Look at the fish I caught," William said, putting two little trout under Sarah's nose before she could get out of the car, "and there's lots more in the stream. If you lie very still on your stomach you can see them in the water."

"I don't think they'll be there for long," said Frances's father. "With William catching them, and the otter I saw further up the stream, the trout don't stand much of a chance."

"Do you see that hill there?" Michael burst in. "I climbed right to the top yesterday. The view is fantastic!"

Sarah and Frances told them about their amazing and wonderful week. While all this talk was going on the fathers cooked a delicious lunch on a barbecue. After they had eaten, the two families sat back quietly and basked in the sunshine.

Sarah's attention, needless to say, was caught by the ponies over the wall. They looked just like Pickles. She struggled to get her wheelchair over the rough ground and finally reached the wall and pulled herself up. She startled the stallion who was standing at the edge of the herd. At a sign from him they all turned and galloped away. "Don't go," cried Sarah to the empty hillside. "I didn't mean to frighten you. Please come back."

At the same time she was thinking, "How beautiful! How wonderful to run free on the hillside like that."

As she gazed after the vanishing ponies she heard her father's voice. "Sarah, can you come here? We have some rather important news we'd like to discuss with you."

Sarah struggled back to join the family.

"We are thinking of moving to a new home," her father told her.

"Can we buy a farm with a herd of Welsh ponies?" asked Sarah breathlessly.

"I am afraid that's out of the question at the moment," her father replied. "Who knows? It might be possible when you are older. But right now, we have the chance to buy a cottage and some land next to Hill Farm. Pickles could live there, and be next door to us."

Sarah thought this over, a happy smile spreading over her face as she thought.

"I'd really like that," she said eventually, "and so would Pickles." Then she added, "Oh, and there is something else I'd really like, too."

"What's that?" asked her mother.

"I'd like another Welsh pony, like Pickles, so that when Mrs. French comes back from America we can drive a pair."

Her father shook his head. "Only a few months ago we thought we couldn't keep one pony. Now you want to have two!"

Nevertheless, the next day they took the farmer who owned the Welsh ponies down to the Center, where he looked at Pickles and the marking on his ear. "That's one of mine, all right," he said. "I should be able to let you have another to match him in looks, but I doubt if I can equal this one's intelligence. I remember this little fellow. I always thought he'd turn out well."

CHAPTER ELEVEN

PICKLES AND SARAH WIN

The next spring, on her return from America, Mrs. French took Sarah to Wales with her to choose a partner for Pickles. The farmer showed them his herd and they picked a matching bay. Mrs. French bought him for herself and named him Pepper. In time, Pickles and Pepper, the two Welsh Mountain ponies, became the focus of attention wherever they went.

Sarah often drove them. She became a familiar figure in the show ring, always the youngest competitor, her chin jutting out in determined fashion as she put the ponies through their paces. Long before she left school she was invited to give demonstrations all over the country. Frances used to go in the carriage with her, while Mrs. French stood at the ringside and cheered them on. The walls of the old

50

stable at the back of Frances's garden were covered with the rosettes they won.

Sarah's family bought the cottage next to Hill Farm shortly after the vacation in Wales, and the whole family enjoyed living there. Sarah never recovered completely from her accident, but when she was riding or driving a carriage no one ever knew how lame she was.

Pickles remained a favorite with all the children who came to Hill Farm to ride, especially the disabled children. Patiently and lovingly he would walk, trot, circle, turn, stop,

walk on, and do whatever he was asked. He was a different pony from the celebrity in the driving world, where he was known for his speed and lightning-fast reactions.

The field he lived in was spacious, and when the wind ruffled his coat, or the spring grass excited him, he would gallop as freely and as happily as he had when he was a foal. He had a favorite place to stand where he could see the gate. He was happy to see Joan, or the Riding for the Disabled helpers, or Frances or Mrs. French. But it was Sarah he always listened for. Whenever he heard her voice calling, "Pickles! Pickles!" or he saw her slight figure limping to the gate, he'd lift his head, prick up his ears and hurry over to greet her. As he licked her hand, she'd often say, "You're the best pony in the whole world, Pickles. You're the one who really helped me."

GLOSSARY

bay a reddish-brown color.

bit a steel piece of equipment for a horse's mouth; part of a bridle.

blacksmith a person who makes new metal shoes for horses.

bridle equipment for leading a horse.

canter a smooth pace, slower than a gallop but faster than a trot.

clear round a clean trip through the obstacle course without a mistake.

colt a young male horse.

foal a newborn horse.

gallop the fastest pace of a horse.

gymkhana a meet to test skills of horses with their riders.

halter a collar or strap for leading a horse; part of a bridle.

mare a mature female horse.

stallion a mature male horse.

trot a slow pace, faster than a walk.

About the Author

Linda Yeatman lives in Cambridge with her husband, three daughters, one dog, and two cats. She is a freelance journalist, and has written a number of books for children.

About the Illustrator

Adriano Goa, who was born in Italy, now makes his home in North London. He has illustrated children's books for many publishers, and has won acclaim for his imaginative drawings of the supernatural.

Other books by Linda Yeatman that you will enjoy reading:
Buttons, The Dog Who Was More Than A Friend
Perkins, The Cat Who Was More Than A Friend

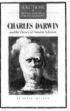
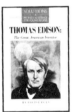